S0-ART-289

by Ray Bradbury

SWITCH ON THE NIGHT

pictures by Leo and Diane Dillon

AN UMBRELLA BOOK

Alfred A. Knopf • New York

For Susan Marguerite and
Ramona Anne with love
— *R. B.*

to E. M. Escher
— *L. D. and D. D.*

AN UMBRELLA BOOK PUBLISHED BY ALFRED A. KNOPF, INC.

Text copyright © 1955 by Ray Bradbury
Text copyright renewed 1983 by Ray Bradbury
Illustrations copyright © 1993 by Leo and Diane Dillon
All rights reserved under International and Pan-American Copyright Conventions.
Published in the United States by Alfred A. Knopf, Inc., New York, and simultaneously
in Canada by Random House of Canada Limited, Toronto. Distributed by Random
House, Inc., New York. Originally published in different form by Pantheon Books, a
division of Random House, Inc., in 1955.

Library of Congress Cataloging-in-Publication Data

Bradbury, Ray, 1920–
Switch on the night / by Ray Bradbury : with pictures by Leo and Diane Dillon.
p.   cm.
"An Umbrella book."
Summary: A lonely little boy who is afraid of the dark is introduced to a whole new
world by his new friend, a little girl.
ISBN 0-394-80486-4 (trade) — ISBN 0-394-90486-9 (lib. bdg.)
[1. Fear of the dark—Fiction. 2. Night—Fiction. 3. Friendship—Fiction.] I. Dillon, Leo,
ill. II. Dillon, Diane, ill. III. Title.
PZ7.B717Sw 1993
[E]—dc20   92-25321

Manufactured in the United States of America   10   9   8   7   6   5   4   3   2

Once there was a little boy
who didn't like the Night.

He liked
lanterns and lamps
and
torches and tapers
and
beacons and bonfires
and
flashlights and flares.
But he didn't like the Night.

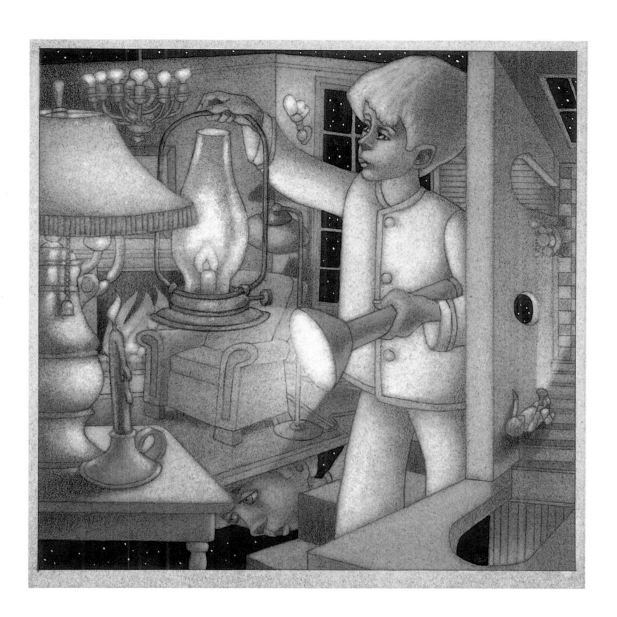

You saw him in
parlors and pantries
and
cellars and cupboards
and
attics and alcoves
and
hollering in halls.
But you never saw him outside . . .
in the Night.

He didn't like light switches at all.
Because light switches turned off
the yellow lamps
the green lamps
the white lamps
the hall lights
the house lights
the lights in all the rooms.
He wouldn't touch a light switch.

And he wouldn't go out to play
after dark.
He was very lonely.
And unhappy.
For he saw, from his window,
the other children playing
on the summer-night lawns.
In and out of the dark and
lamplight ran the children . . .
happily.

But where was our little boy?

Up in his room.

With his lanterns and lamps

and flashlights

and candles and chandeliers.

All by himself.

He liked only the sun.

The yellow sun.

He didn't like

the Night.

When it was time for Mother and Father

to walk around switching off all the

lights . . .

One by one.

One by one.

The porch lights

the parlor lights

the pale lights

the pink lights

the pantry lights

and stair lights . . .

Then the little boy hid in his bed.

Late at night

his was the only room

with a light

in all the town.

And then one night
With his father away on a trip
And his mother gone to bed early,
The little boy wandered alone,
All alone through the house.

My, how he had the lights blazing!
the parlor lights
and porch lights
the pantry lights
the pale lights
the pink lights
the hall lights
the kitchen lights
even the *attic* lights!
The house looked like it was on fire!

But still the little boy was alone.
While the other children played
on the night lawns.
Laughing.
Far away.

All of a sudden he heard
a rap at a window!
Something dark was there.
A knock at the screen door.
Something dark was there!
A tap at the back porch.
Something dark was there!

And all of a sudden someone said "Hello!"
And a little girl stood there in the middle of
the white lights, the bright lights,
the hall lights, the small lights,
the yellow lights, the mellow lights.
"My name is Dark," she said.
And she had dark hair
and dark eyes,
and wore a dark dress
and dark shoes.
But her face was as white as the moon.
And the light in her eyes
shone like white stars.

"You're lonely," she said.

"I want to run with the children outside,"
said the little boy. "But I don't like
the Night."

"I'll introduce you to the Night," said Dark.
"And you'll be friends."
She put out a porch light.
"You see," she said. "It's not switching
off the light. No, not at all!
It's simply switching *on* the Night.
You can turn the Night off and on, just like
you can turn a light off and on.
With the same switch!" she said.

"I never thought of that," the little boy said.

"And when you switch on the Night," said Dark,
"why, you switch on the *crickets!*"

"And you switch on the frogs!"

"And you switch on the stars!

The light stars

the bright stars

the true stars

the blue stars!

Heaven is a house

with porch lights

and parlor lights

pink lights and pantry lights

red lights

green lights

blue lights

yellow lights

flashlights

candle lights

and 1 all lights!"

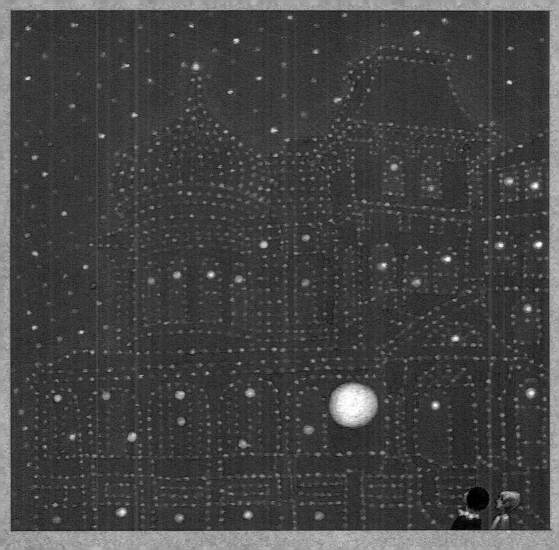

"Who can hear the crickets with the lights on?"
Nobody.
"Who can hear the frogs with the lights on?"
Nobody.
"Who can see the stars with the lights on?"
Nobody.
"Who can see the moon with the lights on?"
Nobody.
"Think what you're missing!
Have you ever thought of
switching on the crickets,
switching on the frogs,
switching on the stars,
and the great big white moon?"
"No," said the little boy.

"Well, try it," said Dark.
And they did.

They climbed up and down stairs,
switching on the Night.
Switching on the dark.
Letting the Night live in every room.
Like a frog.
Or a cricket.
Or a star.
Or a moon.
And they switched on the crickets.
And they switched on the frogs.
And they switched on the white ice-cream moon.

"Oh, I like this!" said the little boy.
"Can I switch on the Night always?"

"Of course!" said Dark, the little girl.
And then she vanished.

And now the little boy is very happy.

He likes the Night.

Now he has a Night switch instead of a light switch!

He likes switches now.

He threw away his candles

and flashlights

and lamplights.

And any night in summer that you wish

you can see him

Switching on the white moon,

switching on the red stars,

switching on the blue stars,

the green stars, the light stars,

the white stars,

switching on the frogs, the crickets, and Night.

And running in the dark, on the lawns,

with the happy children . . .

Laughing.